Dear Parent:

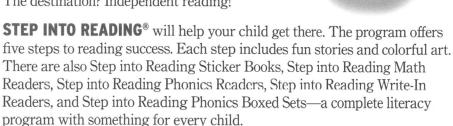

Congratulations! Your child is taking the first steps on an exciting journey. The destination? Independent reading!

STEP INTO READING® will help your child get there. The program offers five steps to reading success. Each step includes fun stories and colorful art. There are also Step into Reading Sticker Books, Step into Reading Math Readers, Step into Reading Phonics Readers, Step into Reading Write-In Readers, and Step into Reading Phonics Boxed Sets—a complete literacy program with something for every child.

Learning to Read, Step by Step!

Ready to Read   Preschool–Kindergarten
• big type and easy words • rhyme and rhythm • picture clues
For children who know the alphabet and are eager to begin reading.

Reading with Help   Preschool–Grade 1
• basic vocabulary • short sentences • simple stories
For children who recognize familiar words and sound out new words with help.

Reading on Your Own   Grades 1–3
• engaging characters • easy-to-follow plots • popular topics
For children who are ready to read on their own.

Reading Paragraphs   Grades 2–3
• challenging vocabulary • short paragraphs • exciting stories
For newly independent readers who read simple sentences with confidence.

Ready for Chapters   Grades 2–4
• chapters • longer paragraphs • full-color art
For children who want to take the plunge into chapter books but still like colorful pictures.

STEP INTO READING® is designed to give every child a successful reading experience. The grade levels are only guides. Children can progress through the steps at their own speed, developing confidence in their reading, no matter what their grade.

Remember, a lifetime love of reading starts with a single step!

To Monk
—F.B.

Visit us on the Web!
StepIntoReading.com
randomhouse.com/kids

Educators and librarians, for a variety of teaching tools, visit us at RHTeachersLibrarians.com

ISBN 978-0-385-37143-8 (trade) — ISBN 978-0-385-37144-5 (lib. bdg.)

Printed in the United States of America 10 9 8 7 6 5 4 3 2 1

DREAMWORKS

MR. PEABODY & SHERMAN

Penny
of the
Pyramids

By Frank Berrios

Illustrated by Bill Robinson

Random House 🏠 New York

Mr. Peabody
is very smart.
He is also
a dog!

Sherman is
a human boy.
He is Mr. Peabody's
adopted son.

Mr. Peabody invented
a time machine.
He wanted to teach
Sherman about history.

Sherman took
his friend Penny
to the past.
Where is she now?

Sherman and
Mr. Peabody have to
find Penny in
ancient Egypt!

Sherman thinks
they should look
in the palace
for Penny.
They want to find
her fast!

Mr. Peabody and
Sherman find Penny.
She does not
want to go home!

Penny likes
ancient Egypt.
She wants to
marry King Tut
and become a queen!

Horns blow
when King Tut
arrives!

Mr. Peabody and
Sherman kneel before
the boy king.

King Tut wants Penny
to be his queen.

King Tut tells
Penny she will be
turned into a mummy
when he dies!

Mr. Peabody and Sherman
try to save Penny.
King Tut has
Mr. Peabody and
Sherman thrown
in a dungeon!

Mr. Peabody finds
a secret tunnel.
They escape!

Mr. Peabody and Sherman almost fall into a huge hole!

A crowd gathers
at the temple
to watch
King Tut marry
Penny.

"Wait!" a voice booms
from a big statue.
"The wedding
must not go on!"

The crowd thinks
the statue is alive!
But it is a trick!
Mr. Peabody is
trying to stop
the wedding.

Suddenly,
the statue breaks!
Mr. Peabody, Sherman,
and Penny use
part of it to get away!

Guards chase them
through the city.

Sherman, Penny, and
Mr. Peabody escape
the guards.

They return
safely to the
time machine.

The trip to ancient
Egypt is over,
but their adventures
through time are
just beginning!